Theft in the Museum

WRITTEN BY
VIRGINIA BOEKENSTEIN

ILLUSTRATED BY
JULIAN PANG

SERIES EDITORS
MITCH AND GJYN O'TOOLE

Theft in the Museum
ISBN: 1 86509 870 1

Written by Virginia Boekenstein
Illustrated by Julian Pang
Copyright © 2005 Blake Publishing and Virginia Boekenstein

Published by Blake Education Pty Ltd
ABN 50 074 266 023
108 Main Rd
Clayton South VIC 3168
Ph: (03) 9558 4433
Fax: (03) 9558 5433
email: mail@blake.com.au
Visit our website: www.blake.com.au

Series publisher: Katy Pike

Highlights! program developed by UC Publishing Pty Ltd
Designer: Luke Sharrock
Series editors: Mitch and Gjyn O'Toole

Printed by Printing Creations

Contents

1. The Theft

The museum was empty. The light from the green, exit sign threw a strange glow across the Persian Room. There were display cabinets everywhere but the lights were switched off. There was not enough light in the room to see what was in the cabinets.

A uniformed, security guard walked through the museum, doing a routine check. He opened the door of each room and shone his torch around. He also had a gun on his belt. Everything was quiet. The museum was deserted.

The guard came to the Persian Room. He thought he heard something inside. He opened the door quickly and shone the torch around inside the room. There was nothing there. The security guard shook his head. "I must be hearing things," the security guard said to himself as he closed the door and walked away.

5

Inside the room, a figure moved in the dark. It jumped off a cabinet and landed softly on the floor. It jumped up onto another cabinet. A dark arm reached high up the wall. A window opened onto the roof. The figure slid silently out. It closed the window as it left. It kept moving silently. It reached the roof and crept away.

Suddenly, the alarm in the museum went off. It was loud and high-pitched. The sound meant something had been stolen from the museum. Lights began to go on all over the building. Torches were flashed into rooms. People were yelling to one another. Doors were slammed. Guards were looking for someone or something.

High above the noise, the dark figure was still moving silently across the roof. It moved onto the roof of the building next door. The figure kept moving steadily forward. It wasn't running, it just moved steadily forward.

The alarm continued to sound. The dark figure moved away from the museum and into the city.

2. Next Morning

The museum was closed for the day because of the theft, but there were still people everywhere.

The Persian Room was closed off with police tape. There was a man in police uniform dusting every surface in the room for fingerprints. Another police officer looked at the list of what should have been in the room. The curator was buzzing around, looking worried.

"This is just horrible," the curator whined. "Who would do such a thing? These artifacts are priceless."

"This whole thing might have been due to a faulty security alarm. We may find that nothing has been stolen," said a tall, well-dressed man who had taken charge.

"Oh no, Detective Walsh, I'm sure something was stolen. I can feel it. Besides," the curator continued, "we have a new security system. It was certainly a thief!"

9

"I don't doubt your security, Ms Smith, I am simply trying to get to the bottom of this," the detective said. "Anything to get this annoying woman to leave me alone and stop pacing," he thought. If this was a faulty security system, he would make sure she heard about it. This was his day off. He was looking forward to spending it at home with his dog! The detective sighed. "Duty calls," he thought. Then he walked away from the agitated woman.

Nothing seemed to have been touched in the room. If everything was intact, why had the cameras in this part of the building shut down? Why had the alarm gone off? The detective glanced around the room. His eyes fell on a window about three metres above the floor.

"Has that window been checked?"

"I don't think so," an officer replied. Walsh moved towards the window, putting on a set of gloves. He grabbed a ladder and climbed up for a better look. Walsh gently pushed the window and it opened.

"Ms Smith," the detective said over his shoulder, "is this window always unlocked?"

"No, I don't think so. There is no need to open it. The museum has central airconditioning."

Walsh took a closer look at the window. This would be a perfect way out if a thief wanted a quick escape. The thief would need to be agile to jump up and out of the window. The window opened onto the museum roof, and from there the thief could slip away unseen. Walsh looked down at the windowsill. His gaze fell on something he had not noticed before.

"I need an evidence bag," Walsh called. Quickly, a junior officer handed up a clear bag to the detective. Walsh carefully placed two cloth fibres into the bag.

"Get these off to be analysed as soon as possible," Walsh said as he handed the bag back to the junior officer. The officer nodded and scurried off. Maybe this was more than a faulty, security system after all.

3. Myths of Persia

"Detective Walsh, I think you should take a look at this," a male voice said. Walsh turned around and glanced in the direction of the voice. The young officer was standing behind one of the display cabinets. The cabinet stood alone and had very old books in it. Walsh climbed down the ladder and walked over to where the officer was standing.

"What is it?" Walsh asked.

"There seem to be small scratch marks on the base of this cabinet." The officer stepped away and Walsh bent down to get a better look.

"We need to open this cabinet and check on the contents." Walsh spoke to no-one in particular. The curator came forward with the key and opened the damaged door. Walsh stepped back and allowed the contents to be checked. Books and ancient pages were taken out and turned over. Each face in the room was gazing at that one freestanding cabinet.

"Everything seems to be here," the curator said, sounding relieved. "Just check that one last book." She pointed to a large book sitting on the bottom self of the cabinet. Walsh stepped forward. He reached in with gloved hands and grasped a large book with heavy, leather binding. The leather was stained and blackened with age. Walsh ran his hand over the cover of the old book. It intrigued him. He opened the cover to look over the pages inside.

Every mouth in the room fell open when he lifted the book from its cover.

"Oh dear!" Walsh said quietly. Walsh flipped through the pages. Where there should have been aged, yellow parchment, there were pages from a phone book. Walsh started to chuckle.

This thief was clever. Walsh tried to control himself. He turned to the curator and asked, "What should this book have been?"

Ms Smith glanced at her list. "It should have been an ancient, Persian text," Ms Smith told the detective. "It was called the Book of Ketab."

"Why would someone steal this book?" Walsh asked.

"Well," Ms Smith explained, "legend says that the book contains descriptions of ancient, Persian treasure. But that is only a myth. No-one has been able to prove it."

"Hang on, let me get this straight," Walsh said quickly. "Some people might think that the book is basically an ancient inventory for the wealth of the Persian Empire."

The curator nodded. "The book is also supposed to contain detailed explanations of the location of the treasure, but that is just a myth," Ms Smith added.

"Who would know about this myth?" Walsh asked. "I think we need to start with finding out about this book." He glanced at the curator. "Where do I go to find out about the Book of Ketab?"

"We generally use the archaeology department at the university. They have two Persian experts. Our contact is Dr Jefferson. I can give you his number."

4. Persian Experts

Ms Smith and Walsh walked to the curator's office. "Has there been any unusual interest in the Persian display?" Walsh asked.

"No, there hasn't been," the curator replied.

"Has anything ever gone missing before?" Walsh asked.

"No, this is the first time anything like this has happened. You really must sort this all out, Detective."

"Yes, I agree, Ms Smith." Walsh said. "Who would have known that this book might be important?"

"Well, people at the university, of course. But they would not steal it. Also a small group of museum employees and anyone who is a budding Persian enthusiast!" The curator grinned with the last comment.

"Ah yes, Persian enthusiasts," Walsh smiled. "Are there many of those?"

21

"Not that I know of," Ms Smith smiled. "Here is the phone number."

"Thank you." Walsh rang the number.

"You have reached the office of Dr Jefferson. I am not available at the moment. If the matter is not urgent, please leave your name and number. If the matter is urgent, please contact my associate Dr Thomas on extension 4678 or at office GL652."

Walsh left a short message. He would have to contact this Dr Thomas.

Walsh parked his car in the parking lot outside the building. He finally found the entrance. "Typical!" Walsh thought. "It's like an archaeological dig. You have to excavate to find the door."

5. Dr Thomas

Walsh pushed the little Help button on the information desk. A middle-aged woman came out. "How can I help you?" she asked.

"I'm Detective Peter Walsh. I'm investigating a theft from the museum. I'm looking for Dr Thomas."

"Yes," she said as she dialled a number. "Dr Thomas, Detective Walsh is here to see you ... It's regarding a theft at the museum ... No, I don't know why you need to be involved ... He is standing right here, I can't tell him to go away ... Yes, I know that you are busy."

Suddenly, the detective's mobile phone rang. "Detective, we just got the analysis on those fibres you found. They could be fragments of a glove that the museum people use when handling artefacts."

"Thank you. Please keep me informed." Walsh said.

Walsh turned to look up the corridor.

A slight figure walked down the corridor.

"I am a very busy woman, Detective. This better be quick," she said bluntly.

Walsh stared at the little woman in front of him. Why had he assumed that Dr Thomas would be a man?

"Are you planning on speaking some time this week?" she asked.

"Oh, I'm sorry," Walsh said. "I'm Detective Peter Walsh."

"What do you want?" she asked.

"Yes, well, I'm invest…"

She cut him off again. "Spit it out, man!" the archaeologist said curtly.

"I will if you give me the chance to. But if you continue to interrupt me, this could take the rest of the day," Walsh said. The woman stared at him. Walsh continued. "An ancient, Persian text was stolen from the museum last night. It is called the Book of Ketab."

"The museum had the Book of Ketab? Why didn't Don tell me?" Dr Thomas sounded surprised.

"Who is Don?" Walsh asked, confused.

The woman's tone suddenly changed. "I'm sorry. I'm Jen Thomas." She held out her hand.

"I'm Peter Walsh" he replied as he shook her hand.

Jen went on. "I'm just a little grumpy. Don Jefferson left this morning without a word. He never tells me when he is going, just leaves me with his work."

Peter was thinking. Where was Dr Jefferson and why had he left so quickly?

"We need to find this book," said Jen. "The place to start would be Don's house."

"If he's away, how do we do that?" Walsh asked.

"Well, I have access to his home!" Jen Thomas said with a smirk.

6. The Son

Jen and Peter pulled up in the car to a large gate and punched in the security code.

"I don't know if Don's son, Kai, is back from the Himalayas yet," Jen said.

They drove up the driveway towards a house on the left of the property.

"It's huge, isn't it?" Jen said. Peter just nodded. "This was a beautiful place, but now it just holds sad memories." Jen went on to explain. "Don's work is his only passion. His wife left him because of it. Now, both Don and Kai spend most of their time away. Don is never home for his son, the poor kid."

Both Jen and Peter got out of the car and headed for the front door. Jen stopped.

"Kai's home," she said and pointed to an expensive-looking car. Jen opened the door and walked in.

31

"Kai?" she yelled. A tall, lanky, young man emerged from a door on the second floor.

"Hey, Jen," he yelled as he ran down the stairs. He grabbed and hugged her.

"How was your trip?" Jen asked.

"Oh, it was great," he replied.

"Kai, what are you wearing?" she asked. He was wearing a cleaner's uniform.

"Dad got me a job at the museum. He wanted to keep me out of trouble," Kai said with a smirk. Then he noticed Peter. "Who's this, Jen?" Kai asked. "Don't tell me you have finally found yourself someone to love."

Peter rolled his eyes. "I'm here on official business." He spoke loudly to interrupt the banter and pulled out his badge. Jen jumped and Kai frowned at the detective.

"And can we please get back to that?" Peter asked. Jen nodded and led Peter up the stairs to the library.

They walked into a huge room whose walls were covered by rows and rows of books. Peter glanced around the room. "Is it strange that Kai is working at the museum?" he asked. Jen thought for a second.

"Actually, I have never known that boy to do a day's work. So yes, I guess it is a little odd," Jen answered.

"Could Kai have had something to do with the theft at the museum?" Peter wondered. He looked at the books in front of him.

"I have no idea what I'm looking for," he said, in defeat. Jen giggled.

"Hang on. I know every book in this library, but I have never seen this one before," she said, pulling a book from the shelf. Peter walked over and glanced over her shoulder at the book she was holding. The book looked like an old folder. Jen opened it and started flicking through the pages.

"Why have I never seen this before?" Jen spoke to herself in disbelief.

7. The Culprit?

"I have never seen these digital photos of maps and Persian books. This one is an image of the book that was stolen." Jen was flicking through the pages quickly now and getting excited. Peter watched her with amusement. "Why didn't Don tell me that he had this? This could be the largest Persian find in this decade."

Peter started thinking. A museum thief would need to know what they were stealing. In this case, they would need to know about Persian artifacts. They would also need to be fit and agile. Don Jefferson had left this morning, right after the theft. He was obviously a suspect. Peter glanced at the photos of the middle-aged man on the desk beside the window. Don Jefferson did not look fit and agile. Then there was Kai. He was fit and agile and had been working at the museum. Kai was another obvious suspect.

Peter glanced out the window, down the driveway and then back at Jen. She was mumbling something about an amazing find and how this could change the understanding of Persian history.

"Jen, Kai's car is gone. Do you think he put it in the garage?" Peter asked. He was looking for an explanation.

"Kai never puts the car away," Jen told Peter absentmindedly. She walked to the door of the library and pressed the house intercom. "Hey Kai, you there?" There was no reply.

Peter was thinking fast. If Kai was the culprit, then he wouldn't stay around the house with a detective about.

Jen glanced back at Peter. "I'm going downstairs to see if he is outside." Peter nodded and followed her.

There was no sign of Kai or his car.

Peter looked around and pointed to the wall on his right. "Is there always a shovel leaning against the house?" he asked.

"No, the gardener always puts his tools back in the shed," Jen answered.

Peter asked, "If you wanted to hide something incriminating on grounds like this, what would you do?"

"I guess you would bury it," Jen answered.

"I think we are going to need some help," Peter said.

The detective pulled his phone out of his pocket. "This is Detective Walsh. I need a search warrant for the Jefferson place and as many officers here as you can arrange, and I need both as quickly as possible." Peter turned to Jen. "They will be here soon. I think we should start over there. That's closest to the shovel."

Jen nodded.

They searched for half an hour but they found nothing. Peter was starting to think that this whole idea was foolish when Jen called out to him from behind one of the trees.

"Peter, there is something buried over here. I'm not sure what it is, but it was buried recently."

Peter hurried over to where she was. He squatted down to get a closer look. "Well, let's have a look, shall we?" He grabbed a pair of rubber gloves from his back pocket, put them on, and started digging with his hands. He found something quite quickly.

"It's a pair of gloves in a plastic bag. One of them is frayed at the end," Peter told Jen. "I wonder if the fabric will match the fibres I found at the museum."

The other police officers began to arrive. Both Jen and Peter stood up and walked to meet them.

"Where would you like us to start?" one of the officers asked Peter.

"I think we have found what we are looking for. You could get the dogs to do a general sweep of the grounds to see if there is anything else out there," Peter said to the officer. He handed over the plastic bag. "Could you please analyse this as quickly as possible? Crosscheck this material with the fibres I found this morning."

The officer nodded and moved off. Peter turned to Jen. "I'm going back to the museum to take another look. Do you want me to drive you back to the university?"

"Can I come with you to the museum?" Jen asked. "Looking around at the Persian exhibit may give me some idea about who would want to buy the stolen book."

At the museum, both Jen and Peter went straight to the Persian exhibit. Jen glanced around the room. The room looked exactly the same as the last time she had been there. You would not know that a theft had happened the night before. That is, if you ignored the police officers bumping around! Jen bent down to look at the cabinet that had held the stolen book. Suddenly Peter's phone rang.

"Walsh here ... Yes ... Are you sure? ... Wonderful ... Thank you very much."

"What is it?" Jen asked.

"The fibres match with the gloves. It looks like the thief is Kai," Peter told Jen.

"I really can't believe that Kai would do anything like this." Jen sighed and went back to studying her cabinet.

Peter walked towards the window that had been the escape path. He looked up and said to himself, "Now all we have to do is find him."